THIS CANDLEWICK BOOK BELONGS TO:

_____

_____

_____

For Davy, best grandpa ever! V. F.   For Michele, who is essential. D. K.

Text copyright © 2004 by Vivian French
Illustrations copyright © 2004 by Dana Kubick

First U.S. paperback edition 2005

Library of Congress Cataloging-in-Publication Data is available.

Library of Congress Catalog Card Number 2003069596

ISBN 0-7636-2520-5 (hardcover)

ISBN 0-7636-2748-8 (paperback)

2 4 6 8 10 9 7 5 3

Printed in Singapore

This book was typeset in Minion Condensed.
The illustrations were done in watercolor, gouache, and pencil.

Candlewick Press
2067 Massachusetts Avenue
Cambridge, Massachusetts 02140

visit us at www.candlewick.com

I Love You, Grandpa

by
Vivian French

illustrated by
Dana Kubick

CANDLEWICK PRESS
CAMBRIDGE, MASSACHUSETTS

Grandpa had come to stay for the weekend. "I'm going to work," Mom said. "Rex, Flora, and Queenie—look after Stanley!"

"Who will *I* look after?"
Stanley asked.
Mom laughed. "You can
look after Grandpa!"
And she waved goodbye.

Goodbye,
Mom.

"Okay," said Grandpa, "what would you like to do?"

"We could go to the playground," Stanley said hopefully, "and swing on the swings!" "I want to play soccer!" Rex said. "I'm good at soccer."

Rex kicked the ball
    to Grandpa, but . . .

Grandpa
missed it.

Stanley tried
to save it,

I'll get it, Grandpa!

but
he fell over.

Oops

"Hmmph," said Rex.
"This is no fun!"
And he went off to
practice by himself.

"Could you twirl my rope for me, Grandpa?" Queenie asked.

"I'll hold the other end,"
said Stanley.

I'll help!

The rope wriggled,
but it didn't twirl.
"Oh dear," said Grandpa.

"My end didn't work either,"
Stanley said sadly.

"I think I'll skip by myself," Queenie said, and she walked away.

"What about jumping?"
Flora suggested.

"How high can you jump,
Grandpa?"

Grandpa couldn't jump very high at all.

"Try again, Grandpa! You do it like this," said Stanley. Grandpa was too out of breath to answer.

"Maybe you've had
enough jumping,
Grandpa," Flora said,
and she went to skip
with Queenie.

"Are you tired, Grandpa?"
   Stanley asked as
   Grandpa sat down
   with a loud sigh.
"Just a little," said Grandpa.

"Poor Grandpa."
Stanley climbed up
beside him.
"I'll look after you. I'll
sing you a song. Mom
always sings me a song
when I'm tired."

Stanley sang Grandpa a song.

I love bees 'cause they go buzz buzz buzz.

And I love little fishies when they go splishy sploshy splishy.

And I love worms when they

wiggle wiggle wiggle.

But most of all I love my grandpa because he is mine

and I love him best of all....

Grandpa listened,
and his eyes slowly closed.
Stanley snuggled up close,
and Grandpa snored
a little snore.
Stanley shut his eyes,
and they slept
peacefully . . .

until Mom came home.

"Ooof!" said Grandpa, rubbing his eyes.

"Stanley!" said Mom. "Have you been tiring Grandpa out?"

"No!" said Stanley. "I've been looking after Grandpa!"

"He's looked after me so well," said Grandpa, "I'm going to take him to the swings."

"We're coming too!" said Rex,
Flora, and Queenie.
"Great!" said Grandpa.
"Are you ready,
Stanley?"

"Hooray!" said Stanley.

"I love you, Grandpa!"

VIVIAN FRENCH has been a storyteller for more than twenty years and has written many acclaimed books for children, including *A Present for Mom*—the first book to feature Stanley. She says, "Dana (and I think she's so clever!) has drawn Stanley to look exactly like my cat, Louis. But he talks and thinks like my daughter Nancy. She's the youngest of four, just like Stanley, and she says it doesn't make life easy!"

DANA KUBICK has designed everything from greeting cards and giftware to teapots and teddy-bear-shaped ice-cream cones. Her work has been widely exhibited, and she has illustrated a number of children's books, including the award-winning *A Present for Mom*. She says, "I fell in love with Stanley, and he took over my life for a while. I nearly expected him to appear around the corner of my drawing table. My friends would ask after him as if he were the newest member of our family. I think, in a way, he is."